P9-BYF-160

1944

Meet Molly

An American Girl

By Valerie Tripp

Illustrations Nick Backes

Vignettes Keith Skeen, Renée Graef

American Girl®

The American Girls

1764

Kaya, an adventurous Nez Perce girl whose deep love for horses and respect for nature nourish her spirit

1774

Felicity, a spunky, spritely colonial girl, full of energy and independence

1824

Josefina, a Hispanic girl whose heart and hopes are as big as the New Mexico sky

1853

Cécile and Marie-Grace, two girls whose friendship helps them—and New Orleans—survive terrible times

1854

Kirsten, a pioneer girl of strength and spirit who settles on the frontier

1864

ADDY, a courageous girl determined to be free in the midst of the Civil War

1904

SAMANTHA, a bright Victorian beauty, an orphan raised by her wealthy grandmother

1914

REBECCA, a lively girl with dramatic flair growing up in New York City

1934

KIT, a clever, resourceful girl facing the Great Depression with spirit and determination

1944

MOLLY, who schemes and dreams on the home front during World War Two

1974

JULIE, a fun-loving girl from San Francisco who faces big changes—and creates a few of her own

Published by American Girl Publishing
Copyright © 1986, 1989, 2000 by American Girl

All rights reserved. No part of this book may be used or reproduced in any manner whatsoever without written permission except in the case of brief quotations embodied in critical articles and reviews.

Questions or comments? Call 1-800-845-0005, visit **americangirl.com**, or write to Customer Service, American Girl, 8400 Fairway Place, Middleton, WI 53562.

Printed in China
13 14 15 16 17 LEO 87 86 85 84 83

All American Girl marks, Molly®, and Molly McIntire® are trademarks of American Girl.

PICTURE CREDITS
The following individuals and organizations have generously given permission to reprint images contained in "Looking Back": p. 53—printed by permission of the Norman Rockwell Family Trust. Copyright © 1943, the Norman Rockwell Family Trust; pp. 54–55—Library of American Broadcasting, University of Maryland; *The Bombing of Pearl Harbor,* by John Hamilton, from the book *War at Sea, 1939–1945,* by John Hamilton, Blandford Press; Bettmann/Corbis; pp. 56–57—AP/Wide World Photos; Wisconsin Historical Society, WHi (X3) 41748; National Archives; Emma Hermann Thieme; Kohler Company Archives; printed by permission of the Norman Rockwell Family Trust. Copyright © 1943, the Norman Rockwell Family Trust; pp. 58–59—Archive Photos; American Red Cross; Bulletin/Temple University Photojournalism Collection.

Cover Background by John Pugh

Library of Congress Cataloging-in-Publication Data

Tripp, Valerie, 1951–
Meet Molly, an American girl
by Valerie Tripp; illustrations, Nick Backes; vignettes, Keith Skeen, Renée Graef.
p. cm.—(The American girls collection)
Summary: While her father is away fighting in World War II, Molly finds her life full of changes as she eats terrible vegetables from the victory garden and plans revenge on her brother for ruining her Halloween.
[1. Brothers and sisters—Fiction. 2. Halloween—Fiction. 3. World War, 1939–1945—United States—Fiction.]
I. Backes, Nick, ill. II. Title. III. Series.
PZ7.T7363Me 1989 [Fic]—dc19 89-3907 CIP AC
ISBN 978-0-93729-581-6 ISBN 978-0-93729-507-6 (pbk.)

7710533

TO MY FAMILY

Table of Contents

Molly's Family and Friends

Chapter One
Turnips 1

Chapter Two
Hula Dancers 17

Chapter Three
Trick or Treat? 29

Chapter Four
War! 36

Looking Back 53

Sneak Peek 61

Molly's Family

Molly
A nine-year-old who is growing up on the home front in America during World War Two

Dad
Molly's father, a doctor who is somewhere in England, taking care of wounded soldiers

Mom
Molly's mother, who holds the family together while Dad is away

Jill
Molly's fourteen-year-old sister, who is always trying to act grown-up

RICKY
Molly's twelve-year-old brother—a big pest

BRAD
Molly's five-year-old brother—a little pest

MRS. GILFORD
The housekeeper, who rules the roost when Mom is at work

LINDA
One of Molly's best friends, a practical schemer

SUSAN
Molly's other best friend, a cheerful dreamer

CHAPTER
ONE

TURNIPS

Molly McIntire sat at the kitchen table daydreaming about her Halloween costume. It would be a pink dress with a long, floaty skirt that would swirl when she turned and swish when she walked. There would be shiny silver stars on the skirt to match the stars in her crown. The top of the dress would be white. Maybe it would be made of fluffy angora, only Molly wasn't sure they had angora back in Cinderella's time. That's who Molly wanted to be for Halloween—Cinderella. All she had to do was

1. talk her mother into buying the material and making the costume,
2. find some glass slippers somewhere, and

3. convince Linda and Susan, her two best friends, to be the ugly stepsisters.

She could probably talk Susan into it. As long as Susan got to wear a long dress, she wouldn't mind being a stepsister. But Linda was another story. If they were going to be fairy-tale princesses, Linda would want to be Snow White because she had black hair just like Snow White's. Linda would want Molly and Susan to be dwarfs. *Probably Sleepy and Grumpy,* thought Molly.

Well, Molly certainly felt like Grumpy tonight. She looked at the clock. She had been sitting at the kitchen table for exactly two hours, forty-six minutes, and one, two, three seconds. She had been sitting at the kitchen table, in fact, ever since six o'clock when Mrs. Gilford, the housekeeper, called everyone to supper.

Molly had smelled trouble as soon as she walked into the kitchen. It was a heavy, hot smell, kind of like the smell of dirty socks. She sat down and saw the odd orange heap on her plate. She made up her mind right away not to eat it. "What's this orange stuff?" she asked.

Mrs. Gilford turned around and gave her what

Molly's father used to call the Gladys Gilford Glacial Glare. "Polite children do not refer to food as *stuff*," said Mrs. Gilford. "The vegetable which you are lucky enough to have on your plate is mashed turnip."

"I'd like to *re*turn it," whispered Molly's twelve-year-old brother Ricky.

"What was that, young man?" asked Mrs. Gilford sharply.

"I like to *eat* turnips," said Ricky, and he shoveled a forkful into his mouth. Eating turnips—or anything alive or dead—was no hardship for

Ricky. If it could be chewed, Ricky would eat it. Quick as a wink, all his turnips were gone.

That rat Ricky, thought Molly. She looked over at her older sister Jill. Jill was putting ladylike bites of turnip in her mouth and washing them down with long, quiet sips of water. Almost all of the horrible orange stuff was gone from her plate.

Molly sighed. In the old days, before Jill turned fourteen and got stuck-up, Molly used to be able to count on her to make a big fuss about things like turnips. But lately, Molly had to do it all herself. Jill was acting superior. This new grown-up Jill was a terrible disappointment to Molly. If that's what happened to you when you got to be fourteen, Molly would rather be nine forever.

The turnips sat on Molly's plate getting cold. They were turning into a solid lump that oozed water. With her fork, Molly carefully pushed her

meat and potatoes to a corner of her plate so that not a speck of turnip would touch them and ruin them. "Disgusting," she said softly.

"There will be no such language used at this table," said Mrs. Gilford. "Furthermore, anyone who fails to finish her turnips will have no dessert. Nor will she be allowed to leave the table until the turnips are gone."

That's why Molly was still at the kitchen table facing a plate of cold turnips at 8:46 P.M. *None of this would have happened if Dad were home,* she thought. Molly touched the heart-shaped locket she wore on a thin chain around her neck. She pulled it forward and opened it up to look at the tiny picture inside. Her father's face smiled back at her.

Molly's father was a doctor. When American soldiers started fighting in World War Two, Dr. McIntire joined the Army. Now he was somewhere in England, taking care of wounded and sick soldiers. He had been gone for seven months. Molly missed him every single minute of every single day, but especially at dinner time.

Before Dad left, before the war, Molly's family never ate supper in the kitchen. They ate dinner in the dining room. Before Dad left, back before the war, the whole family always had dinner together. They laughed and talked the whole time. Now things were different. Dad was gone, and every morning Molly's mother went off to work at the Red Cross headquarters. Very often she got home too late to have dinner with the family. And she spent at least an hour every night writing to Dad.

When a letter came from Dad, it was a surprise and a treat. Everyone gathered and listened in silence while Mrs. McIntire read the letter aloud. Dad always sent a special message to each member of the family. He told jokes and drew funny sketches of himself. But he didn't say which hospital he worked in or name any of the towns he visited. That wasn't allowed, because of the war. And even though Dad's letters were long and funny and wonderful, they still sounded as if they came from very far away. They were not at all like the words Dad spoke in his deep-down voice that you could feel rumbling inside you and filling up the house. Molly used to be able to hear that voice even when she was up in her room doing homework.

When Dad called out, "I'm home!" the house

Even though Dad's letters were long and funny and wonderful, they still sounded as if they came from very far away.

announced. "The soldiers need the tin in those cans more than we do. From now on, we will grow, preserve, and eat our own vegetables. It's the least we can do for our fighting boys."

All summer long, Mrs. Gilford had tended her Victory garden. She wore a stiff straw hat, Dr. McIntire's gardening gloves, and knee-high black rubber boots. Everyone, even little Brad, had helped her. Molly had worked in the Victory garden every Tuesday morning from ten to eleven o'clock. She had crawled on her hands and knees through rows of green seedlings, pulling weeds. The rows were as strict and straight as soldiers on parade. Each one was labeled with a colorful seed packet on a stake. The seed packets showed fat carrots, plump red tomatoes, and big green peas.

Call VEGETABLES INTO SERVICE

But by fall, after months in the hot sun, the pictures on the seed packets had faded away. The packets hung on the stakes like limp white flags of surrender. Mrs. Gilford's Victory garden had not been quite as victorious as she had hoped. All but the toughest vegetables had been beaten by the dry summer. The carrots were thin and wrinkled. The tomatoes were hard as nuts. The peas were brown. But that did not defeat Mrs. Gilford. Mrs. Gilford would never give up and open a tin can. She had a rather successful crop of radishes, lima beans, and turnips, so that's what they would eat.

As Molly stared at the turnips on her plate, she remembered Mrs. Gilford saying, "Wasting food is not only childish and selfish, it is unpatriotic. Think of your poor father off in some strange land. Maybe he didn't have enough to eat tonight. And you turn up your nose at fresh turnips. You will not leave this table until those turnips are gone. Completely."

Now it was almost nine o'clock. It was getting cold in the kitchen. Molly was lonely. She was tired of thinking about how unpatriotic she was. She looked at the turnips, lifted a tiny forkful, and put it in her mouth. Just then Ricky burst through the swinging kitchen door.

"How do you like eating old, cold, moldy brains?" he teased. Then he ran out.

Molly swallowed the turnips fast, then gulped down a whole glass of water. Old, cold, moldy brains was exactly what the turnips were like. She would not eat one speck more.

"Ricky, you rat!" she said. "I'm going to get you!" She started to get up from the chair.

From behind the door Ricky chanted, "Nyah, nyah, nyah-nyah nyah! You can't leave the table. You haven't finished your turnips!"

"Ricky, stop it!" yelled Molly. But Ricky was right. The turnips were still on her plate and she was stuck. To make matters worse, Molly heard her mother calling good-bye to the car pool she rode with from Red Cross headquarters.

Now Mom will be mad at me, too, thought Molly. *Now she'll never make a Cinderella dress for my Halloween costume. Now everyone in the house will be mad at me for making Mom upset. And all because of these terrible turnips.*

Mrs. McIntire walked in the back door, looked at Molly, looked at the plate, and knew immediately what had happened. "Well, Molly," she said. "I see we had the first turnips from the Victory garden for dinner tonight."

"Mom," said Molly, "I hate turnips. I know I do. And Mrs. Gilford says I can't leave the table until

I eat them. I'll be here until I die, because I will never eat these. Never. I really mean it."

"I see," said Molly's mother. "Do you mind if I join you for a while? Not until you die, of course—just while I have a cup of tea. And while I'm heating up the stove, why don't I reheat those turnips for you? They certainly don't look very good when they're cold like that."

"It won't help," said Molly.

But Mrs. McIntire scooped up the turnips and put them in a frying pan. "I'll just smooth out these lumps. And I think we can spare a little bit of our sugar and butter rations to add to the turnips," she said, almost to herself. "And a little cinnamon, too."

Soon a delicious, spicy aroma filled the kitchen. The kettle whistled, and Mrs. McIntire made her tea. She spooned the turnips back onto Molly's plate and put the plate in front of Molly.

The hot steam from the turnips warmed Molly's face and clouded her glasses. She took a deep breath, raised a small forkful to her lips, and tasted it. It wasn't so bad. In fact, it was pretty good—sweet, cinnamony, and kind of like applesauce. It

felt good going down, not at all like old, cold, moldy brains. She ate another forkful.

Mrs. McIntire sat down with her tea. "When I was about your age," she said, "my mother made sardines on toast for dinner one night. Little oily dead fish on toast! I refused to eat them. But my mother said I could not leave the table until the sardines were gone. *Gone* was exactly what she said. So when she wasn't looking I put each sardine, one by one, into my napkin. Then I stuck my napkin into my pocket. When my mother saw my empty plate she was surprised, but she excused me from the table.

"I used to play checkers with my father every night after dinner. That night it was very hard to concentrate on the game. Our two cats, Bessy and May, yowled and meowed and climbed all over me. They smelled the sardines. Finally, when I had one hand on Bessy and the other hand on a checker, May pulled the napkin out of my pocket. The sardines spilled out all over the rug. Bessy and May gobbled them up."

"Oh, Mom!" laughed Molly.

"Oh, Molly," sighed Mrs. McIntire. "Sometimes

*"The war **has** changed things," said Mrs. McIntire.*
"But some things are still the same."

we have to do things whether we like it or not. There aren't always cats around who will eat the sardines." She reached across the table and brushed Molly's bangs out of her eyes. "I know this war is hard on you children. And I know you miss your father. I miss him, too."

"Everything is so different with Dad gone," said Molly. "Nothing is the way it used to be anymore."

"The war *has* changed things," said Mrs. McIntire. "But some things are still the same. Isn't Ricky still Ricky?"

"He sure is," said Molly. "Still dumb old Ricky."

"And you are still my olly Molly," said Mrs. McIntire. "And I am still me." She gave Molly's hand a squeeze.

Molly smiled. The turnips were gone. Mom was not mad. Mrs. Gilford wouldn't think that Molly was ruining her war effort.

"Thanks, Mom," she said as she gave her mother a hug. She walked carefully up the stairs to bed, pretending she was wearing a long, floaty pink skirt that swished as she took each step.

CHAPTER TWO

HULA DANCERS

The next morning dawned all gold and blue and windy. *Perfect Halloween weather,* Molly thought as she woke up. At breakfast Mrs. Gilford didn't say anything about the turnips, but she made French toast, which was a sign that all was forgiven.

It was Thursday, and Molly's friends Linda and Susan were coming home with her after school. They were going to plan their Halloween costumes. They had made a secret pact not to discuss their ideas until they got to Molly's house. "Someone might copy us if they heard our idea," said Molly. Linda and Susan agreed. Besides, it was fun to have a secret pact—it was sort of like being soldiers and keeping battle plans away from enemy spies.

As they walked home after school they met Alison Hargate, who was one of their classmates. She asked, "What are you three going to be for Halloween?"

"We can't tell," said Molly. "It's a surprise."

"Oh," said Alison.

Linda said, "But it's *great*. It's really a great idea."

Susan chimed in, "Yes! It's wonderful! We're going to have the best Halloween costumes ever."

Alison looked impressed. Molly was a little worried. The girls hadn't even agreed on what they were going to be. The mystery was making their costumes get a lot of attention. They were really going to have to make good costumes, or else everyone would tease them.

"What are you going to be, Alison?" Molly asked.

"Oh, probably an angel," said Alison. "My mother said I could wear her white satin dressing gown, and she's already made me some gold wings and a halo."

Molly, Linda, and Susan were suddenly very

quiet. Molly was jealous. She was sorry she had even asked Alison. An angel! What a great idea! Alison was sure to look wonderful with a halo over her golden hair.

It was very hard to have Alison for a friend. Alison was an only child, and her parents were rich and gave her everything that anyone could want. Alison didn't mean to brag about the things she had, but just by telling the truth she managed to make everyone resent her.

"My mother doesn't even have a dressing gown, much less a white satin one," said Linda glumly. "All she has is a brown terry cloth bathrobe. I know she'd never even let me wear that."

"Well," said Molly to Alison, "all I can tell you is that *our* idea is much more . . . um . . . original than an angel."

"Yeah, I know an angel is kind of boring," said Alison quickly. "It was my mother's idea. She made the wings and all."

dressing gown

"Well, see you later, Alison," said Molly as she and Linda and Susan hurried away. It made them uncomfortable when Alison started being so *nice.*

When the girls got to Molly's house, they went into the kitchen for a snack.

"Hello, Mrs. Gilford," they said together.

"Hello, girls," answered Mrs. Gilford. She was watering the parsley plants she'd started to grow on the kitchen windowsill. "There are some apples in the bowl on the table. Help yourselves, but take your apples outside, please. It's too nice a day to be cooped up in the house."

"Thank you, Mrs. Gilford," the girls said as they went to sit on the back steps in the sunshine.

Ricky was out back, too, shooting baskets at the hoop on the side of the garage. He was trying to set a world record for making the most baskets without missing.

As the girls munched their apples, Susan said, "Gee, I think an angel is a good idea. Why don't we be angels, too?"

"Absolutely not," said Molly. "Do you want Alison to think we stole her idea?"

"Alison wouldn't mind," said Susan.

"I know," said Molly. "But *I* would mind. We can think of something just as good."

"Like what?" asked Linda.

"Well," replied Molly slowly, as if she had just thought of it for the very first time. "How about Cinderella and the two ug—I mean, the two stepsisters?"

"Oooooh," said Susan. "Cinderella!"

"Who gets to be Cinderella?" Linda asked immediately.

"We don't have to decide that right away," said Molly. "Let's . . . uh . . . let's wait and see who has the best ball dress, and that's the one who will be Cinderella. The other two will be stepsisters."

"I don't think it's fair," Linda stated. "Who wants to be an ugly stepsister?"

"You're all ugly step *sitters* today," teased Ricky. "Get it?"

"Cut it out, Ricky," said Molly. Ricky went back to shooting baskets.

"I think it's a good idea," said Susan. "My sister Gloria just gave me an old prom dress of hers. It's sort of green, with a big petticoat and shiny gold threads at the bottom of the skirt. I'll wear that."

"Sort of green," Ricky mocked. "Lima bean green is what you mean."

"Ricky, go away," said Molly. But she was thinking that Susan's dress sounded perfect for Cinderella. And it had two very big advantages over Molly's floaty pink dress with the white angora top. Susan's dress really existed, and Susan already had it. Being an ugly stepsister was not at all what Molly had in mind.

"Wait a minute," she said. "Maybe Linda is right. Maybe it's not fair. Maybe we should all be exactly the same thing, like the Three Musketeers."

"You'd be perfect as the Three Little Pigs," said Ricky. "Or you could be the Three Bears. How about the Three Stooges? Or the Three Kings of Orient?" He began to sing in a loud, teasing voice:

"We three kings of Orient are,
Tried to smoke a rubber cigar,
It was loaded, it exploded . . ."

"STOP IT!" yelled Molly.

And suddenly, Ricky did stop. His face turned red. He bounced the basketball under his legs, then behind his back. He leaned casually against the garage and twirled the ball on the tip of one finger.

The girls turned around to see who he was showing off for. It wasn't Mrs. Gilford or even Mrs. McIntire. Nobody was there except Jill and her new best friend Dolores. They were walking up the driveway, carrying their school books.

Dolores was wearing a bright blue sweater just the color of her eyes. She had a wide, white smile, like a movie star in a toothpaste ad. She stopped and flashed her smile at Ricky.

"Hi, Rich," she said.

"Rich!" snorted Molly. Lately, Ricky had been telling everybody to call him Rich because it sounded more like a soldier's name than Ricky did.

"Hi, Dolores," he squeaked in a very odd voice. He turned quickly, jumped, and sent the basketball swishing through the basket just as Dolores went in the door.

Molly, Linda, and Susan looked at each other and dissolved into giggles. It was crystal clear to them what Ricky's problem was. Ricky-Rich had a crush on Dolores! The three girls started to chant:

"Ricky and Dolores up in a tree,
K-I-S-S-I-N-G!
First comes love,
Then comes marriage,
Then comes Ricky with a baby carriage!"

Ricky threw the basketball at the girls. But they hopped up and out of the way, making loud, slurpy kissing noises. "Ricky has a crush!" they chanted. "Ricky loves Dolores!"

"Hi-i-i, Do-lor-esss," Molly squeaked, imitating Ricky. She pretended to kiss the basketball.

"Eeeeeuuuuwwww!" Linda and Susan shrieked.

"You'll be sorry!
*You'll **pay** for this!" Ricky called.*

Ricky jumped on his bike. As he sped past the girls he called, "You'll be sorry! You'll *pay* for this!"

The girls just giggled until they ran out of breath and their stomachs hurt. Finally, they got serious again and went back to the question of what to be for Halloween.

"We could be the princesses of England," suggested Linda.

"There are only two of them, Elizabeth and Margaret Rose. One of us would have to be their mother," said Molly.

"How about being nurses?" asked Susan. "We could all wear capes."

"That's what we did *last* year!" Linda and Molly said together.

They considered being acrobats, three Alices in Wonderland, ice skating stars like Sonja Henie, or the Three Blind Mice. No one could get very excited about being a blind mouse, and anyway, Mrs. McIntire overheard them and said she absolutely did not have time to make a mouse costume for Molly. "And besides," added Mrs. McIntire, "in wartime I don't think it's right to use good material for Halloween costumes."

Molly, Linda, and Susan groaned. They knew Mrs. McIntire was right.

"But I've got another idea, girls," said Mrs. McIntire. "I'll show you how to make grass skirts out of newspaper and crepe paper. Then you can be hula dancers."

"Well," replied Susan, "my sister Gloria taught me how to make flowers out of crepe paper, just like they did to decorate for the prom. We could string them together and make flower necklaces and headdresses."

"I think my father has an old ukulele," said Linda. "It doesn't have any strings, but it will look good."

"It's too bad it's so cold, because I know my mother will make me wear socks and shoes and a sweater on top," said Susan. "But at least the flower necklaces will hide most of the sweater."

So the girls decided to be Hawaiian hula dancers for Halloween.

Soon after that the streetlights went on, which meant Linda and Susan had to go home. They agreed to meet back at Molly's house after school the next afternoon, to make their costumes. Then they would all go trick-or-treating together. Afterwards, Linda and Susan would spend the night at Molly's so they could talk about how wonderful their Halloween had been.

By the time she went inside to supper, Molly had completely forgotten Ricky's threat to make them all sorry. She was too busy practicing her hula.

CHAPTER THREE

TRICK OR TREAT?

The grass skirt made out of newspaper and crepe paper was not exactly as glamorous as the pink floaty skirt Molly had imagined. But it was quite long, and it did make a nice rustling noise as she walked. Besides, making the skirts had been lots of fun. Mom came home from Red Cross headquarters early, just so she could help. She put on a record of Hawaiian songs. Then they all sat in the den, cutting the newspaper into strips. They covered the newspaper with strips of green crepe paper. Mom sewed all the paper onto long pieces of cloth to tie around their waists like aprons. Susan showed them how to make crepe paper flowers that were big and colorful. They made

strings of the paper flowers to use as necklaces and bracelets. Mrs. McIntire even squirted some of her perfume on them.

By the time they were ready to go out trick-or-treating, Molly, Linda, and Susan were caught up in the excitement of Halloween and very pleased with their matching hula outfits.

"Adorable! You look as cute as buttons!" said Dolores. She and Jill bobby-pinned the big flowers into the girls' hair.

"When I get back from taking Brad trick-or-treating, I'll take your picture to send to Dad," said

Mrs. McIntire. Brad was wearing a sheet. He was going as a ghost. "Ricky, I'll want a picture of you, too."

"Okay, Mom," said Ricky. He was dressed as a pirate. Ricky was a pirate every year.

It was a windy night, but not too cold, so the girls rolled down their socks and pushed up the sleeves of their sweaters. The wind made their skirts ripple so that they looked graceful and pretty, just like real grass skirts.

They saw Alison when they went to the Silvanos' house down the street. Her angel outfit was perfect. She had a flowing white satin robe with fluffy white feathers at the neck and cuffs and all down the front. Her wings and halo were covered with gold glitter.

"Hula dancers!" Alison sighed with envy when she saw them.

Molly was very pleased. *They* had made Alison jealous. "Your outfit is good, too," Molly said. "You really look like an angel." She felt like being nice. In fact, it would probably be fun to trick-or-treat with Alison, except Alison's mother always went with her.

"Hawaiian hula dancers!" Mrs. Hargate was saying. "What charming costumes, gals! And homemade, too! Aren't you clever?" The girls just smiled and hurried away.

"Really," Linda said later, "you almost have to feel sorry for Alison with a mother like that!"

"I know," said Molly. "Wouldn't it be awful to have a mother who doesn't know that the whole *point* of Halloween is to go out and walk around the neighborhood with your friends, and not with her?"

Because of the war, most people did not have any sugar to spare, so the girls did not get as many candies and cookies as last year. Nevertheless, their brown paper bags were soon bulging with apples, doughnuts, molasses kisses, peanuts, and popcorn balls. The Hargates' maid was giving out Tootsie Roll Pops, which were the best treats.

Two families, the Pedersons and the Ruckstein, asked the girls to do a trick before they got their treats. So the girls did a hula, waving their arms and singing the Hawaiian song they learned in school. Linda strummed her stringless

ukulele. It was a big hit. The Pedersons, especially, clapped and clapped. They gave the girls each two glasses of cider.

Linda believed in eating her treats along the way, so her bag was not as full as Susan's and Molly's when the girls finally walked back up the driveway to Molly's house. Molly was humming the Hawaiian song, Linda was unwrapping a popcorn ball, and Susan was making her skirt swish and sway. They were almost to the back door when a huge splash of water poured down on top of them and a hose sprayed straight at them.

"AHHHH!" Molly yelled. The water flooded around her feet in cold gushes. She felt as if she was drowning in a waterfall. Her bag of treats burst, the popcorn balls floated in puddles, the doughnuts turned to spongy globs, the apples rolled away down the sidewalk. Linda and Susan were gasping. Their paper flowers were flattened. Their skirts were hanging in shreds. The green dye from the crepe paper was dripping down their legs onto their socks.

When the water finally stopped, Molly's hair was stuck to her forehead, her hands were full of

A huge splash of water poured down on top of them and a hose sprayed straight at them.

melting paper flowers, and most of her hula skirt lay in soggy ribbons in the driveway.

"Ruined! Wrecked! Completely wrecked!" sobbed Molly. "Who would play such a mean trick?"

Then the girls heard Ricky singing in a low, slow, steady voice:

"I see London,
I see France,
I can see your underpants!"

"Ricky," yowled Molly, "I'll get you for this! You ruined everything! You'll be sorry—you wait! You'll be *really* sorry."

Ricky threw the hose down and ran off. The girls just stood there in the driveway, stunned with surprise and sputtering with anger. Maybe they shouldn't have teased Ricky about Dolores, but who ever would have expected him to get back at them in such a terrible, mean way?

Finally Linda said, "I'm freezing!"

Molly said, "You two go on inside. I'll clean up this mess. Then we've got some planning to do. We have to teach Ricky a lesson he'll never forget."

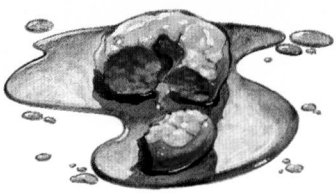

CHAPTER FOUR

WAR!

A while later, Linda, Susan, and Molly sat in Molly's room in their pajamas. Still pink and warm from their baths, wrapped head to toe in big white blankets, they looked like three rosy polar bears. The girls were whispering together on Molly's bed when they heard Mrs. McIntire returning with Brad.

"Would you hula dancers like some cocoa?" Mrs. McIntire called up to the girls.

"Okay, Mom," called Molly. "We'll be right down."

"Good!" said Susan. "Now we can tell her what Ricky did!"

"No!" Molly said quickly.

"Why not?" asked Susan.

"I don't want to be a tattletale," said Molly. "Besides, she'd be too easy on him. We have to take care of Ricky ourselves."

The girls walked slowly into the kitchen. There at the table sat Ricky, still in his pirate costume. He was sipping cocoa and looking as innocent as a kitten. Molly, Linda, and Susan sat as far away from Ricky as possible.

"Well, girls," said Mrs. McIntire. "How was your Hawaiian Halloween?"

"Fine," said the three girls all together, but it sounded as if they meant just the opposite.

Mrs. McIntire looked puzzled. "Just 'fine'? That's all?" she asked. "And why are you all in your pajamas already? I wanted to take your picture to send to Dad. What happened to your costumes? And your bags of treats?"

"They got wet," said Molly.

"Wet?" asked Mrs. McIntire. "How?"

The girls looked at each other. "By a hose," said Susan. "Ricky—"

"We walked into a hose. By mistake," said Molly quickly, before Susan could finish.

"Who would be using a hose on a windy Halloween night?" asked Mrs. McIntire.

The girls said nothing. Finally Molly said, "Just someone."

Mrs. McIntire frowned. "Molly McIntire," she said. "I have the distinct feeling that I am not being told the whole story."

Molly stared into her cocoa cup. Ricky pushed his chair back from the table.

"Perhaps *you* can tell me what happened, Ricky," said Mrs. McIntire.

"Me?" squeaked Ricky. He fiddled with the handle of his pirate dagger. "I didn't . . . I mean . . . I mean . . ."

"Go on, Ricky," said Mrs. McIntire.

"Well, it was just a joke, Mom," said Ricky. "Just a joke on the girls. You know, a Halloween joke? Trick or treat?"

"A *mean* trick," muttered Linda.

"What did you do?" asked Mrs. McIntire, staring steadily at Ricky.

"I just got a little water on their costumes," said Ricky.

"A *little* water?" squealed Molly. "You dumped

*"Perhaps **you** can tell me what happened, Ricky," said Mrs. McIntire.*

pails and pails of water all over us, Ricky!"

"You squirted us with a *hose!*" Susan added indignantly.

"You ruined our costumes and all our treats!" said Linda.

"Is that true?" asked Mrs. McIntire.

"Yes!" exclaimed all the girls.

"Ricky?"

"Yes, ma'am," muttered Ricky. He looked at his feet.

Mrs. McIntire was quiet. Then she said, "Ricky, that was a very mean thing to do. I'm ashamed of you, treating your sister and her friends that way. I think I can say that your father would be ashamed of you, too. I'm going to punish you just as I think he would have punished you." Mrs. McIntire sighed. "You are to apologize to these girls. Then you are to give your bag of Halloween treats to Linda, Susan, and Molly to share. You may keep one treat, and only one, for yourself. I'm going upstairs to put Brad to bed now, and while I'm gone I want you to apologize. Is that clear?"

"Yes, ma'am," said Ricky.

"Girls, after Ricky apologizes, I want you to go

to bed. I'll come in later to say good night," said Mrs. McIntire as she left with Brad.

After she had gone, Ricky muttered, "Sorry." Then he shoved his bag of Halloween treats into Molly's hand and ran out of the kitchen.

As the girls trudged up to bed, Linda whispered, "You were right, Molly. She was way too easy on him."

"Yeah!" said Susan. "Except for the part about your father being ashamed."

"He wrecked our Halloween, and he's hardly suffering at all!" added Linda.

"Well," said Molly as she flopped on her bed, "we'll just have to think up a plan to make Ricky *really* suffer."

"Let's let the air out of his bicycle tires," suggested Susan.

"Not bad enough," said Molly.

"We could put frogs under his pillow," said Linda. "Dozens and dozens of frogs."

"Yeah, but then we'd have to catch the frogs," Susan pointed out.

"Eeeeeuuuuwwww!" they all shrieked.

"We could disguise our voices and call him up on the telephone," said Susan. "We could pretend we're Mrs. Mobley, his teacher, and say he has to stay after school every day next week for being bad."

"No," said Molly. "That's no good. It doesn't embarrass him in front of anybody. We have to really embarrass him in front of lots of people, or in front of someone he'd hate to be embarrassed in front of, like Mom, or . . ."

"Or Dolores!" said Linda.

"Yes, that's it!" said Molly. "Embarrass him in front of Dolores!"

"But how?" asked Susan.

The girls were quiet for a minute. Molly was still mad—as mad as a wet hen, her father would say. She could remember Ricky chanting,

"I see London,
I see France,
I can see your underpants."

Underpants? Dolores? Molly thought. Then she smiled to herself.

"I think I have a plan," she said to Linda and

Susan, "but all three of us have to cooperate or it won't work."

The next morning was Saturday. The breakfast table was crowded. Dolores, who had spent the night with Jill, was talking about the movie they were all going to see that afternoon. Ricky came to the table last. His hair was slicked back with water. *That's probably so Dolores will notice him,* thought Molly, but she didn't say anything. She wouldn't say anything to Ricky—she was still too mad about what he had done the night before.

Susan was the first to start the plan to get back at Ricky. She asked Mrs. McIntire for three big brown bags. "We need them to hold our Halloween treats," she said with a look at Ricky. Mrs. McIntire gave her the bags.

Linda had a harder job to do. She had to keep Ricky out of his room for a while after breakfast. "Can I watch you shoot baskets?" she asked Ricky. "I want to learn how."

"Girls can't play basketball," answered Ricky rudely.

"Ricky!" said Mrs. McIntire. "What an unfriendly thing to say! You march outside like a gentleman and show Linda how to shoot baskets. She is our guest."

"Yes, ma'am," said Ricky.

He and Linda went outside. Mrs. McIntire walked with Brad to the mailbox around the corner to mail a letter to Dad. Dolores followed Jill up to her room to listen to records.

As soon as Jill's door closed, Molly and Susan dashed into Ricky's room. They flung open the top drawer of his dresser and dumped his underwear into a brown bag. They turned his laundry bag upside down on the floor, gathered the underwear and dirty socks from the pile, and stuffed them into the other two bags. They made one last quick check to be sure the room did not look disturbed before they rushed back to Molly's room.

The window in Molly's room looked out over the back door and driveway, where Ricky was shooting baskets and Linda was watching. Molly opened the window wide. "Okay, go on," she whispered to Susan.

"I can't do it," hissed Susan. "I'm too scared. And it's lying."

"Go *on,* Susan," said Molly. "You *have* to do it. Linda and I will never speak to you again if you don't. Just cross your fingers, then it's not a lie."

"Okay," said Susan. She went and knocked softly on Jill's door. Jill and Dolores were inside practicing the rhumba.

"What do *you* want?" Jill asked Susan.

"Well," said Susan, "I thought you'd like to know that Russ Campbell is at the corner in his car. He told me to run in here and tell you two—I mean *ask* you—if you wanted to go for a ride with him."

"Russ Campbell?" Jill and Dolores shrieked. Russ Campbell was the senior football star at Montgomery High School, where Jill and Dolores were freshmen. A ride in Russ Campbell's car was a dream come true for them.

"Oh, how do I look?" asked Jill in a panic.

"You look fine," said Dolores. "Gosh, I'm glad we curled our hair last night!"

"Let's go!" said Jill. "Let's go before Russ changes his mind."

"Okay!" said Dolores. The girls galloped down the stairs, but just before they went out the back door they slowed down, patted their hair, smoothed their skirts, and straightened their shoulders.

Susan ran back to Molly's room. "Get ready! They're on their way outside!"

Seconds later, just as Dolores and Jill strolled out the back door, Molly and Susan leaned way out the window, yelled as loud as they could, and turned the big brown bags upside down. Underwear and T-shirts filled the air like giant, floppy snowflakes. Dozens of socks tumbled down. A T-shirt got caught in the basketball hoop. A dirty sock landed on Jill's shoulder. Some plaid undershorts landed right on Dolores's head.

"What's *this?*" asked Dolores in disgust as she lifted the underwear off her head with the very tips of her fingers.

Molly, Susan, and Linda chanted:

"I see London,
I see France,
Those are Ricky's underpants!"

Underwear and T-shirts filled the air like giant, floppy snowflakes.

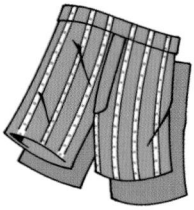

"RICKY!" screeched Jill. "That's REVOLTING!" She threw the dirty sock at Ricky. "And I suppose that business about Russ Campbell was part of the joke, too! Of all the stupid, *childish* things to do!"

"But I *didn't*," Ricky wailed.

"Here, Ricky," Dolores interrupted. She was still dangling the undershorts from her fingertips. "I believe these cute little underpants belong to you, don't they?" As she tossed them to Ricky, she winked at Jill. Suddenly, they both started to laugh. They laughed so hard they had to sit down on the back steps and laugh some more. Ricky got very red in the face. He ran around frantically collecting his socks and underwear.

Finally Dolores gasped, "Come on, Jill. Let's go to my house. At least we can be pretty sure we won't be showered with some little kid's underwear!" Jill and Dolores started down the driveway, still laughing at Ricky.

Molly called out the window, "There's YOUR Halloween trick or treat, Ricky!"

"I'll get you!" Ricky yelled back. "You'll be sorry! This is *war!* This is really war! I'll—"

Suddenly Ricky stopped. He stood still in the driveway. Jill and Dolores stopped, too.

Molly and Susan leaned out of the window to see why. There was Mrs. McIntire, standing at the end of the driveway with Brad. Her face was as hard and cold and white as a marble statue. "Uh-oh," said Susan. She slid down to the floor next to Molly.

Mrs. McIntire looked up at the window. "Come down here at once, girls," she said sternly. "Jill and Dolores, I want you to hear this, too."

In seconds, everyone stood on the back steps. Molly's legs were shaky. No one said anything. Then Mrs. McIntire began to speak.

"Until there are no more tricks in this house, there will be no more treats," said Mrs. McIntire. "Instead of going to the movies, Ricky, you will spend your day raking the yard. Make sure you rake up the Halloween mess you made—all the bits of costumes, all the ruined food. Susan, Linda, and Molly, you will spend your day doing Ricky's laundry. I want everything washed, hung out to dry, folded, and put away by the end of the afternoon. Jill and Dolores, you will take care of Brad."

Mrs. McIntire paused. She looked straight at Molly, then straight at Ricky. "I suppose these tricks you have been playing on each other don't seem very serious to you. But they are mean, childish, and wasteful. I'm disappointed in you, but more than that, I'm sad and discouraged. If we can't get along together, who can?"

Molly looked at Ricky. Ricky looked at his mother. "This fighting *has* to stop," Mrs. McIntire went on. "This is exactly what starts wars—this meanness, anger, and revenge. Two sides decide to get even and end up hurting each other. There's war and fighting enough in the world, and I won't have any more of it in our house. Is that understood?"

Everyone mumbled, "Yes, ma'am."

"All right, then," said Mrs. McIntire. "Get to work." She went inside.

Molly stood up and faced Ricky. "Give me your un—uh, your things," she said.

"Here," said Ricky. "I think that's all of them." He pushed the bundle into her arms.

"Okay," said Molly. "Listen, we didn't—I mean, we didn't want to keep fighting with you, exactly. We were just mad. We wanted to embarrass you. We shouldn't have done it. I'm sorry. I really am."

"It's okay," said Ricky. "I guess I deserved it." He began to smile a little. "Your trick was mean, but you know, it was funny, too." He laughed. "I'm kind of glad not to be fighting against you any more. You three have pretty good ideas, even if you are a bunch of triple dips. I guess it's better to be on your side than to be your enemy."

Molly grinned. "Thanks, Ricky," she said. She

and Linda and Susan went inside.

It wasn't so bad doing Ricky's laundry. Molly, Linda, and Susan pretended they were three Cinderellas *before* the ball. So, in a way, Molly got to be Cinderella for Halloween after all. And later, when the girls went outside to hang the laundry on the clothesline, Mrs. McIntire came out to help them.

"It sort of looks like an underwear tree, doesn't it?" she said when they were finished. She smiled down at Molly, who turned and gave her a hug. Her mother was right: it was much better not to be fighting.

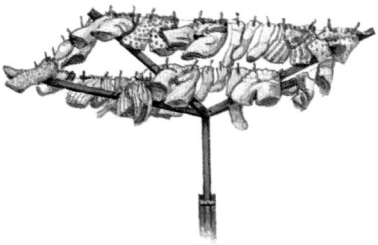

LOOKING BACK

AMERICA IN *1944*

If you lived in Molly's world you probably would have had a big radio in your living room. You'd listen to it for fun, just as you watch television today. You'd wait to hear each new episode of *The Green Hornet.* You'd listen for the train whistle on *I Love a Mystery.* And your whole family would probably try to answer "The $64 Question." Many families like Molly's were listening to the radio on December 7, 1941, when they heard the announcer say:

> "We interrupt this program to bring you a special news bulletin. This morning, Japanese planes attacked the American military base in Pearl Harbor."

Japanese bombers attacked Pearl Harbor, an American naval base in Hawaii.

Many American soldiers and sailors were killed in the bombing of Pearl Harbor. People all over the United States were angry and wanted to fight back. They felt the faraway war they'd been hearing about for the last two years wasn't so far away anymore.

World War Two had begun long before December 7, 1941. In Europe, the German army had already attacked peaceful countries like England and France. Germany's leader was a dictator named Adolf Hitler. Hitler and his followers, the Nazis, wanted to stretch their power until they controlled the world. After Pearl Harbor was bombed, Americans joined the war to stop the Germans and the Japanese.

Adolf Hitler

Thousands of American men volunteered to fight. They became soldiers, pilots, and sailors. They drove ambulances and tanks. They worked as doctors, mechanics, and cooks. Women joined the armed forces,

Men and women served their country.

too. They worked in military hospitals and offices. They drove jeeps, ordered supplies, and nursed the wounded.

Almost every family in the United States had to say goodbye to someone who went to war. People missed their relatives and worried about them. Like Molly and her family, they wondered where the people they loved were and whether they were safe. Soldiers could write letters to their families, but they weren't allowed to say much about what they were doing. And their letters were *censored*—parts of them were cut out—so that enemy spies could not read them and learn where Americans were ready to fight.

When American soldiers joined the fighting, American

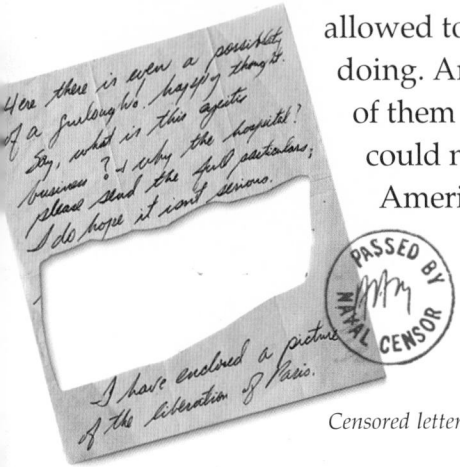

Censored letter

American factories made war equipment.

factories "went to war," too. Car factories made airplanes and tanks instead of new cars. Clothing factories made uniforms and tents instead of dresses. Shoe factories made boots for marching instead of shoes for playing. Factories that once made toys were changed to make war equipment.

Before the war, most American women did not have jobs. But as men went away to fight, more and more women went to work in offices and factories. They built and tested airplanes, repaired train engines, and ran businesses. Women proved they could do any job that needed to be done.

Even people who did not go off to fight said they were "fighting on the *home front*." People on the home front changed the way

This painting of "Rosie the Riveter" showed that women could do hard factory work.

Vacant lots were often turned into large Victory gardens for the whole neighborhood.

they lived so that the United States could win the war. They drove their cars less so there would be plenty of gas for airplanes, tanks, and army trucks. They stopped buying food in cans so the metal could be used for guns and bullets instead. They raised their own food by planting Victory gardens so that the food farmers grew could go to the soldiers.

People working on the home front often volunteered to do important work without pay. They knitted socks and blankets, made bandages, and packed boxes of food to send to the soldiers. Some worked for the Red Cross, like Molly's mother, collecting blood to help wounded soldiers.

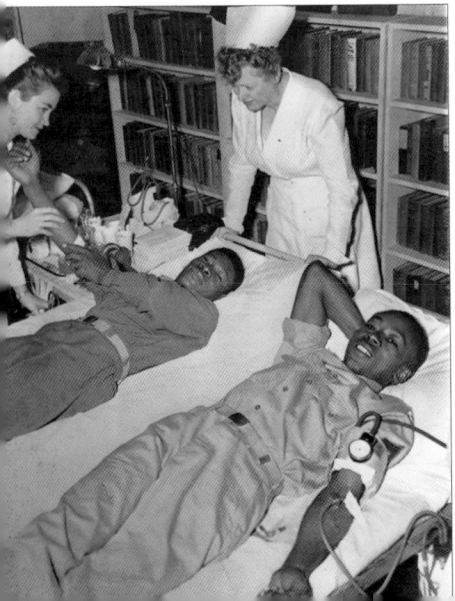

Americans helped the Red Cross by giving blood.

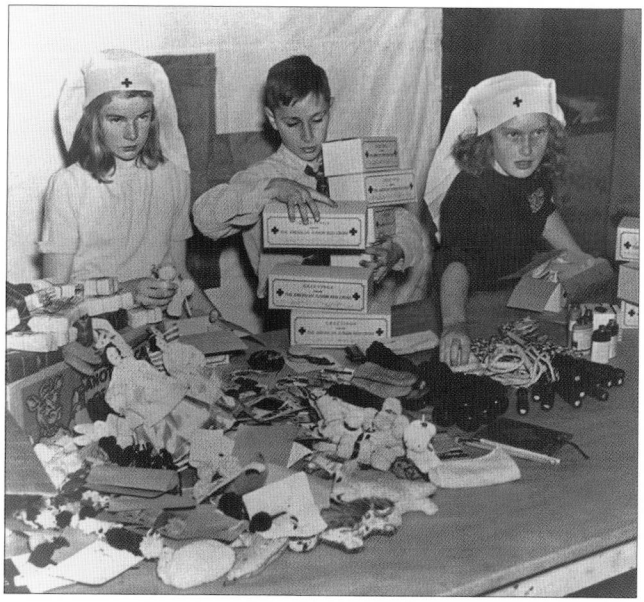

World War Two was hard for people who fought and for people on the home front. Millions of people were killed. Many more were wounded. Americans who stayed at home were often frightened and lonely, but they were also proud of their men and women in uniform. To show their pride and love, people hung blue stars in their windows, one for each family member who was away at war. If someone was killed, the family hung a gold star in the window.

Americans were also proud of what their country was doing. They were willing to make the sacrifices they did because they believed that if they could win the war, the world would be a better place for everyone.

Families hung a blue star flag in the window for every family member who was away at war.

A SNEAK PEEK AT

Molly LEARNS A LESSON

Molly wants to win the Lend-a-Hand contest at school—and she's positive that keeping her plan a secret is the way to win.

The garage was cold, especially compared to the warm kitchen. It was dark, too, because the only light came from the door at one end of the storage room and a window at the other end. The girls couldn't stand up straight except in the very middle of the storage room because the ceiling was sloped just like the sides of a tent.

The storage room smelled of dust, mothballs, and dried-up paper. It was filled with things waiting to be fixed up, thrown out, or needed again. There was a big trunk with one latch broken, boxes full of books and games with pieces missing, a tarnished tennis trophy, a chest of drawers with a mirror on top that made you look green and speckled, a box labeled "Curtains—Too Short," and a roll-top desk with no drawers. Everything looked ghostly because everything was covered with a gray blanket of dust.

The girls had pushed two old love seats together, face-to-face, right under the window. The love seats were not very comfortable because the springs and padding had fallen out of the bottom of them. But they had high, curved backs, so when they were pushed together they made a sort of boat that floated in a dusty sea.

Linda climbed aboard first. "Knitting!" she groaned. "I'm going to be terrible at this project. I *hate* knitting. Everything I ever knitted came out looking like a piece of chewed string."

"Oh, I think knitting is fun," said Susan. "And socks are cute."

"Have you ever knitted a sock?" asked Molly.

"Well, no," said Susan. "But I've seen people do it."

"Yeah, well it's *hard,*" said Molly. "I've watched Mrs. Gilford do it. You have to use three needles sometimes, and count stitches, and purl, and turn the heel, and lots of other complicated things."

Susan looked at Molly for a while. "I'll bet you don't like it just because it's Alison's idea," she said. "You're jealous because Alison won the multiplication bee and Miss Campbell gave her the gold badge today, and you did the worst of anybody."

"That's not true!" said Molly.

"It is too!"

"I'm going to be terrible at this project.
*I **hate** knitting," Linda groaned.*

"It is not!"

"It is too!"

"Cut it out," said Linda. "It doesn't matter whose idea it is. I still can't knit."

"I think we should do another project," said Molly.

"We can't," said Susan. "All the girls are doing socks. It's our Lend-a-Hand project. Miss Campbell would be mad at us. *Everyone* would be mad at us if we didn't do socks."

"Listen," said Molly. "Those girls are crazy if they think they can each knit even one pair of socks by Monday. They can't possibly do it. The whole third grade will look terrible. They'll be grateful to us if we do another project. Miss Campbell will be proud of us."

Susan was doubtful. "Well, I don't know."

"Look, you want to win the contest, don't you?"

"Yes, but—"

"Well, believe me, there's no way the third grade girls can ever win by knitting socks. It's up to us. We have to do another project and win the contest for the third grade girls." Molly was firm.

"You make it sound so easy to win," said Linda. "What other project can we do that would be so great? Build a fighter plane or something?"

Susan giggled. "We could become spies and go on a mission and steal top secret information from the enemy."

"Hey!" said Molly. "That's it! We sort of *could* be secret agents."

"What do you mean?" asked Susan.

"Well," said Molly, "we're secret agents because nobody knows what we're doing, right? Just us three. And our mission is our project. Only instead of stealing information, we can collect something, something like—"

"Tops! Bottletops!" interrupted Linda. "Get it? *Top* Secret. We'll be Top Secret Agents."

"Yes!" said Molly. "That's it! We'll collect bottletops for scrap metal. They use scrap metal to make tanks and battleships and things, so it's good for the war effort. We'll collect at least a hundred bottletops, and we'll surprise everybody in school on Monday. And we'll win the contest, and Miss Campbell will be pleased with us."

"Top Secret Agents!" said Susan. "Just like in the

movies. We can wear matching clothes. You know, spy clothes—dark pants and dark shirts—and send notes in a secret code, and have a secret hide-out."

"Right here!" said Molly. "This can be our hide-out."

"We should have a secret handshake, too," said Linda. "And we can never show anybody what it is."

"And we can't tell anybody what our secret project is," said Molly. "We have to be sworn to secrecy."

"Okay, let's swear," said Linda. "Come on! A solemn oath!" She raised her right hand. Molly and Susan did, too. "I promise never to tell anyone—"

"Shhh!" Molly interrupted. "I hear something!"

"What is it?" asked Susan. "An enemy spy?"

Molly waved to her to be quiet. She crept over to the window. "It's Alison! Alison Hargate is knocking on the kitchen door!"

"I want to see," said Linda. She joined Molly at the window.

"Get down!" Molly commanded. She and Linda knelt by the window.

"Hey, look!" said Linda. "Alison has a big white envelope in her hand."

They looked down at Alison from their hide-out. They saw Mrs. Gilford come to the door, wiping her hands on her apron. Alison showed Mrs. Gilford the envelope. Mrs. Gilford nodded and squinted up at the garage, then pointed right at the window. The girls ducked. They heard footsteps coming toward the garage.

"She's coming this way!" whispered Linda. "She's coming to find us."

"Quick! Hide!" Molly hissed.

"But—" said Susan.

"Hurry *up*," ordered Molly. "If she sees us it will ruin everything!" She slithered under one of the love seats. Linda hid behind a trunk. Susan knelt in a corner, then popped up like a jack-in-the-box and ran over to hide under the roll-top desk.

Molly's heart was pounding. It smelled musty under the couch, and the broken springs dug into her back. After what seemed like a long time, she heard the door open. All she could see were Alison's

feet. The feet came into the room and stopped.

"Molly?"

Molly held her breath.

7710533
RUTH CHAFFEE ELEMENTARY SCHOOL

READ ALL OF MOLLY'S STORIES,
available at bookstores and *americangirl.com.*

Ruth L. Chaffee
Elementary School
Library Media Center
Newington, CT 06111